Life Under the Sea
Pufferfish

by Mari Schuh

Ideas for Parents and Teachers

Bullfrog Books let children practice reading informational text at the earliest reading levels. Repetition, familiar words, and photo labels support early readers.

Before Reading

- Discuss the cover photo. What does it tell them?
- Look at the picture glossary together. Read and discuss the words.

Read the Book

- "Walk" through the book and look at the photos. Let the child ask questions. Point out the photo labels.
- Read the book to the child, or have him or her read independently.

After Reading

- Prompt the child to think more. Ask: Have you ever seen a pufferfish? Was it puffed up?

Bullfrog Books are published by Jump!
5357 Penn Avenue South
Minneapolis, MN 55419
www.jumplibrary.com

Library of Congress Cataloging-in-Publication Data

Schuh, Mari C., 1975– author.
  Pufferfish / by Mari Schuh.
     pages cm. — (Life under the sea)
  "Bullfrog Books are published by Jump!."
  Summary: "This photo-illustrated book for beginning readers describes the physical features and behaviors of pufferfish. Includes picture glossary and index."— Provided by publisher.
  Audience: Ages 5–8.
  Audience: K to grade 3.
  Includes bilbiographical references and index.
  ISBN 978-1-62031-190-5 (hardcover: alk. paper) — ISBN 978-1-62496-277-6 (ebook)
  1. Puffers (Fish)—Juvenile literature. I. Title.
  II. Title: Puffer fish. III. Series: Bullfrog books.
  Life under the sea.
  QL638.T32S38 2016
  597.64—dc23
                                        2014042736

Editor: Jenny Fretland VanVoorst
Series Designer: Ellen Huber
Book Designer: Lindaanne Donohoe
Photo Researcher: Jenny Fretland VanVoorst

Photo Credits: All photos by Shutterstock except: age fotostock, 1, 11, 12–13; Alamy, 4, 16–17, 23br; Nature Picture Library, cover; SuperStock, 18–19; Thinkstock, 15.

Printed in the United States of America at Corporate Graphics in North Mankato, Minnesota.

To my kindergarten teacher, Mrs. Trunkenbolz—MS

Table of Contents

Puffed Up

A pufferfish looks for food.

It finds coral to eat.

Pufferfish have teeth.
They look like a beak.
They bite the coral.
Chomp! Chomp!

Oh no!
A sea snake!

This puffer is slow.
It can't get away.
But wait!

It takes in water.
Gulp!

It puffs up.

Now it is big.

It is round.

It is hard to eat.

Most fish have scales.

14

But pufferfish do not.
They have stretchy skin.

Stay away!

They have poison.

Spines keep them safe, too.

Some puffers are bright.
The colors tell enemies
to stay away.

This one is dull.

It hides.

Now it is safe.

Parts of a Pufferfish

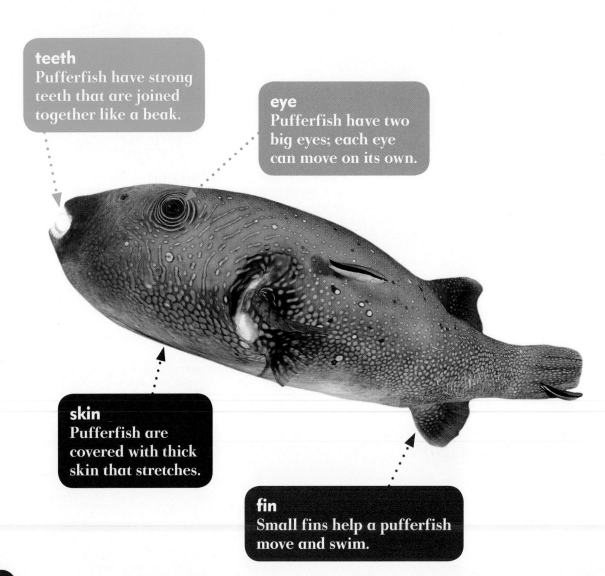

teeth
Pufferfish have strong teeth that are joined together like a beak.

eye
Pufferfish have two big eyes; each eye can move on its own.

skin
Pufferfish are covered with thick skin that stretches.

fin
Small fins help a pufferfish move and swim.

Picture Glossary

beak
The hard, horny parts of an animal's mouth.

scales
Small, overlapping hard pieces of skin.

coral
Hard skeletons of small sea animals.

spine
A sharp point on a pufferfish's body.

Index

To Learn More

Learning more is as easy as 1, 2, 3.

1) Go to www.factsurfer.com

2) Enter "pufferfish" into the search box.

3) Click the "Surf" button to see a list of websites.

With factsurfer.com, finding more information is just a click away.